D0567028

Midnight Soup
and a Witch's Hat

ALSO BY DORIS ORGEL

My War with Mrs. Galloway
Whiskers Once and Always

MIDNIGHT SOUP AND A WITCH'S HAT

BY DORIS ORGEL

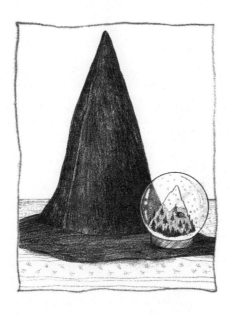

Illustrated by Carol Newsom

Viking Kestrel

For Laura

VIKING KESTREL
Viking Penguin Inc., 40 West 23rd Street, New York, New York 10010, U.S.A.
Penguin Books Ltd, 27 Wrights Lane, London W8 5TZ (Publishing & Editorial) and
Harmondsworth, Middlesex, England (Distribution & Warehouse)
Penguin Books Australia Ltd, Ringwood, Victoria, Australia
Penguin Books Canada Limited, 2801 John Street, Markham, Ontario, Canada L3R 1B4
Penguin Books (N.Z.) Ltd, 182-190 Wairau Road, Auckland 10, New Zealand

Text copyright © Doris Orgel, 1987
Illustrations copyright © Carol Newsom, 1987
All rights reserved
First published in 1987 by Viking Penguin Inc.
Published simultaneously in Canada
Printed in the United States of America by Haddon Craftsmen, Bloomsburg, Pennsylvania
Set in Sabon Roman
1   2   3   4   5   91   90   89   88   87

Library of Congress Cataloging-in-Publication Data
Orgel, Doris.   Midnight soup and a witch's hat.
Summary: Having anticipated a whole week with her
father in Oregon, Becky arrives to find that she has
to share her dad with his friend Rosellen and her
spoiled six-year-old daughter.
[1. Fathers and daughters--Fiction]   I. Newsom, Carol,
ill.   II. Title. PZ7.0632Mi   1987
[Fic]   87-8328   ISBN 0-670-81440-7

Contents

Me and Dad

The whole thing started when I was over at the Noonans and Michael got mad at his father. His father had asked him to watch Mandy for a while and to keep her entertained.

Mandy's a year and a half. She sat in her high chair and banged on it with a spoon, making a big racket.

Michael gave her Cheerios. "Eat 'em, they're yum."

Mandy ate one. "Yum." She tries to say whatever Michael says. She picked up another Cheerio. But instead of eating it, she dropped it.

Michael said, "Oops."

"Oops," said Mandy, and gave him a great big smile. She's crazy about Michael. And she asked, "Mo 'oops'?"

Michael said, "Sure, go ahead, more 'oops.' "

Just then Mr. Noonan came in, right when Mandy threw down all the Cheerios, "Oops, oops." The bowl, too. Good thing it was plastic, so it didn't break. But the milk and sugar made the floor all gloppy.

"That's some way of keeping your sister entertained," Michael's father said, and handed him a broom. "Okay, now clean up the mess."

Michael said, "No fair. Mandy's the one who made it."

"You put her up to it. Go on."

Michael started to sweep. The Cheerios stuck to the broom bristles. When he stooped down to unstick them, his father gave him a whack on the behind—not too hard, but still.

"Ouch! Hey, that hurt!" Michael slammed the broom down.

Mandy started crying.

Mr. Noonan picked her up. "Thanks a lot, Michael, you were some big help."

Michael's face got all red and he swallowed, hard. "I tried to be," he said in this really mad voice. "Most guys I know who have kid sisters wouldn't even bother. Come on, Becky, let's get out of here." He grabbed my hand and pulled me to the door.

I said, "So long, Mr. Noonan. So long, Mandy, see you later."

We went upstairs to 5G, Mom's and my apartment.

Michael said, "How unfair can a guy's father get? Oh wow."

"Yeah. Want to play Parcheesi?"

"No."

"Concentration? Car race?"

No and no. He just wanted to go on and on about how mad he was.

"As mad as a tiger with a knot in his tail?" Our class made up animal comparisons like that in Language Arts one time.

"I'm just plain old mad." Michael was in no mood to kid about it. "Sometimes I hate him. Don't you?"

"I don't know him that well."

"Not mine, dumbhead. Yours. I mean, don't you sometimes hate your father?"

"No."

"Oh no, of course not, I forgot, you wouldn't."

I thought, Look out, here it comes. Michael and I have been friends for ages. We really like each other. But when he feels bad about something, he'll try to make me feel bad, too. Just so he'll have company.

Here it came: "Your father is never around. You never see him long enough to get good and mad at him. Sorry I said anything." But he didn't sound sorry one bit.

"My father is *so* around. He's already visited us three times."

"Yeah, but just on holidays. Holidays don't count."

"They do so. And anyway, I'm going out there."

"Oh yeah? When? You've been saying that all year."

My father lives in Portland, Oregon. He moved out there three years ago, after he and Mom got divorced.

Michael's wrong about holidays. They count. Do they ever!

The first time Dad came to visit was on a Thanksgiving. He and I went into Manhattan

early in the morning to see the Macy's Day Parade live instead of just on TV. He's six-foot two, and I sat on his shoulders. I saw really well from up there.

It was windy, it was freezing. It even started to snow. I had a woolly hat on that covered my ears. Dad's ears felt like ice, though, and were turning red. So I got this idea: I didn't need my mittens. I could keep my hands warm by putting them in my pockets. So I stuck my mittens over Dad's ears. He said, "Thank you, Boodle, that feels good."

Pretty soon some other dads near us were wearing *their* kids' mittens like that. "Hey," said Dad, "we may have started a whole new style in ear wear for men!"

Anyway, now his ears felt nice and warm. And we stayed till the end of the parade. We saw every float, right up to Santa Claus.

Later we went to Grandma Sonia's for Thanksgiving dinner, just like in the old days.

While Dad carved the turkey, there was a moment when nobody talked. My friend Kyra thinks when that happens it means an angel is flying through the room. I think it's because people are thinking things they can't say out loud.

Grandma Sonia went "Ahem" and asked me the question she asks me every year. "So, Becky, what do you feel thankful for the most?"

"Um—" I looked at Mom. She looked down at her plate. I couldn't catch her eye. It was like an invisible fence went up around her. That happens sometimes when Dad's there, or when she's thinking about him.

I looked at Dad. He concentrated on carving.

Grandma Sonia said, "I take back the question. It's too personal."

So I didn't have to say it out loud. But they knew it anyway. The thing I felt most thankful for was that Dad was there. For me, having him around was what that whole Thanksgiving was about.

The next year Dad came in December. Decorations were up everywhere. Of course, because it was nearly Hanukkah and Christmas. But to me the biggest reason why everything looked all glittery and shiny was that Dad was there.

Last time he visited was in September. My birthday's September 4th, same day as Labor Day last year. We went to the fireworks in Prospect Park and Dad said into my ear, in an important voice, like a newsman on TV: "Today we cele-

brate the arrival in the world eight years ago of
the one and only Becky Suslow!"

Fine with me. And when the huge ones ex-
ploded, the ones that fill the whole sky full of
flower-showers, I said, "Those are to celebrate
that you're home."

Of course our apartment is really not his home
anymore. He slept on the living-room couch. He
said he didn't mind the cracks between the cush-
ions. And he kept his clothes in the closet in the
foyer.

On the last night of his stay, I got up to go to
the bathroom around 2 or 3 A.M. I knew it was
around that time by the shade of purplish-dark
the sky was, and because no people were down
on the street. When I came out, I saw the light on
in the kitchen. I smelled onions. Sometimes when
my dad can't sleep, he makes Midnight Soup. That's
what he was doing.

My cat, Whiskers, smelled it, too. She was still
alive then. She followed me into the kitchen.

Butter sizzled in the big pot. Chopped-up onions sizzled in the butter. We stirred them around
till they turned buttery brown. We poured in water
and put in all this stuff: a lamb bone; leftover
chicken gravy; a cut-up frankfurter; parsley; cel-

ery; carrots; and dill. When it bubbled up, we lowered the flame and let it simmer. The longer soup like that simmers, the better it's going to taste.

Dad and I ate some for breakfast. It tasted great.

Then I had to go to school. And he went to the airport. By the time I got home, he was halfway across America.

I ate a bowl of Midnight Soup that night, and every night for a week. Usually I get tired of anything I eat every day. But Midnight Soup tastes better each time. The only trouble with it was, it made me miss him even more.

Wrong Number?

The day Michael had the fight with his father, I invited him over for dinner. Mom was going out, with her friend Pete. Pete's a veterinarian. I hated him at first. I thought it was his fault that Whiskers died. But it really wasn't. Pete's okay, I'm getting used to him.

Michael and I ate with Mrs. Galloway. After dinner, she went in the living room to watch *Dallas*. She stays glued to the TV when that show is on.

Good thing, or she'd have yelled at us: "Get

out of there, the bathroom's not a playroom!" We were getting ready for a naval battle on the high seas. Michael had brought his eleven plastic fighter planes. We fit them onto an old flat, wooden boat of mine. We divided up the rest of my boats into two navies. We filled up the tub and began.

"Hey, we made a rule, you can't put your arm in that deep," Michael said. Too late! I'd already zoomed my submarine to the surface and bashed it into the aircraft carrier. The carrier capsized with a big splash and all his fighter planes landed in the water.

Michael can be a sore loser. He started in again, "So when are you flying out to Portland, like you said, huh?"

"I don't know yet. Soon, though."

" 'Soon?' Don't you know when grown-ups say 'soon', they mean in a hundred years?"

"Not my father. When he says 'soon,' he means it. I'll prove it to you. I'll call him up, right now."

We went into the kitchen. I picked up the phone.

Mom has a rule about that: no long-distance calls unless I ask first. But then we have this other rule. Well, it's not a rule, exactly. It's more like an understanding: if I really need to talk to Dad, and it's very urgent, then I could go ahead and call.

I pushed the numbers: 1, then 503, the area code for Oregon, then Dad's number.

Michael sat there munching on raisins and nuts Mrs. Galloway'd left out for us. He looked pleased with himself. Like he'd dared me to call, and that's why I was doing it.

The phone in Oregon rang two times. I thought, Come on, Dad!

"Hi, who's this?" said a little-bitty voice.

I asked, "Who're you?"

"Hope."

Oh no, not again! That happened one time before. I must have gotten the same wrong number as that other time when I fell into the trap and asked, "Hope who?" And she'd answered, "Hope you go soak your head. Ha, ha."

This time I beat her to the punch. "Hope I never hear your voice again!" *Bang,* I hung up.

Michael asked, "What was that all about?"

"Just a wrong number."

He wanted me to try again.

I didn't feel like it. I still wanted to talk to Dad, but not with Michael there.

On nights Mom goes out, I sleep in her room. Then I move into mine when she comes home, and it gives me a chance to see her.

She has a phone next to her bed. I tried again. I touched the numbers extra carefully.

This time Dad answered.

"Dad, listen, I've been wondering, when can I come out to visit you?"

He said all the things I'd already heard before: "It's a really long trip. . . . You're pretty young to fly that far by yourself. . . . And it costs a lot of money." More than he sometimes earns in a whole month!

"I know, but Dad, I've been wanting to, for so long! How about if Mom helps pay for my ticket? I bet she would." Mom makes more money than Dad does. She's a doctor. Dad is a terrific painter, and someday everybody'll want to buy his paintings, but he isn't famous yet. So he also paints houses, outside and in, to earn money to live on.

He said, "I'll think about it."

"Dad! That's no answer!"

"Easy, Boodle, don't get so upset." And he asked, "What's wrong?"

"Nothing. I just want to see you, and see what it's like where you live. I want to go with you to all the places you've sent me postcards of. I want to do things together. When can I?"

"Becky, honey, I want to see you, too. I miss you all the time. It's just that things are a little bit unsettled right now."

"You mean on account of Rosellen?" Rosellen is *his* friend, sort of the way Pete is Mom's friend. Only, Rosellen moved into his house.

I was always proud of Dad for giving me straight answers. Now, though, all he'd say was, "It's hard to explain on the phone."

I asked, "When will things be more settled?"

He didn't know.

"You sound like you don't want me to come that much."

"Hey, I sure do. And you know it, Becky-Boo." That's his nickname for me when I'm sad and blue. "I'll tell you what, I'll talk it over with your mom one of these days, and—"

"Dad, don't say 'one of these days,' it doesn't sound like you!"

"Okay, you're right. Becky, I promise that you'll come out here. Just at this moment, though, I can't say exactly when."

"Yeah. Maybe in ten years. Or maybe when it's Hanukkah and Christmas in July."

"Please don't be sarcastic."

"I can't help it!" And I nearly hung up the phone. Except, we once promised we'd never do that. So I said, "Good night."

And he said, "Good night, Boodle. See you soon."

Flying to Portland!

A week later, on June 15th, when I came home from school, Mrs. Galloway stood in front of our house and waved an envelope at me. "Wait till you see what just came for you, Special Delivery!"

The envelope had a border of red, white, and blue, with clouds and airplanes in the corners. I tore it open.

"Airplane tickets! I'm flying to Portland on July 1st! And back on the 8th, a whole week out there with Dad!" I grabbed Mrs. Galloway around the waist, "Yippee!"

She's usually pretty old-fashioned and doesn't approve of acting "wild" or "making a spectacle of yourself." Well, she grabbed me around my waist, right there on the sidewalk. And we swung around, like in a dance. That's how happy she was for me.

Of course Mom was glad for me, too, when I told her. Just not dancing-around-the-room glad, and she got a little quiet, the way she sometimes does when things come up about Dad.

When I was little, I used to think it was just because she missed him a lot and, well, maybe one of these days he'd move back to Brooklyn and everything would be just the way it used to be.

One time, I was around six, Mom and I were sitting in the blue velvet chair with daisies, where we have our private times. And Mom guessed what I was thinking: Why didn't they get back together? And she told me please not to expect that to happen. Because it just wasn't going to, no matter how much I wished it would. I still remember, she pulled me onto her lap. She laid her cheek next to mine. I dug my nose into her hair, to smell the lilacs-and-hospital smell. Mom-perfume, I used to call it.

"But you're lucky, Becky," she'd said, and

hugged me to her. "Feel how close we are? Well, when you're with your father, you can be just as close to *him*. And that'll never change."

Anyway, the day my airplane tickets came, and Mom and I were sitting together, I was so excited wondering what it would be like and what Dad and I would do together. Mom stayed pretty quiet.

After a while she said, "You know about this friend of his, Rosellen—"

"Yes, I already know, she's living in Dad's house. Mom, what if I don't like her? What if she doesn't like me?"

Mom said it would all work out and I shouldn't worry.

"Guess what, I'm flying to Portland on July 1st," I told Michael on the way to school next morning.

"Yeah, and I'm climbing Mount Everest."

"No, it's true! I'll even tell you my seat number, it's 7A. On Flight Number 423. It'll leave from Kennedy at 3 P.M., our time, and it'll land in Portland at 5:45 P.M., their time."

"Good for you." He stared up at the sky. A plane flew over, real fast, and left a long white trail behind it. Michael sucked his breath in.

"Boy, I wish *I* was in one of those."

That's the way it is, when something great happens to somebody else. You wish it was happening to you. You can't help it. Probably everybody's like that.

Like, when we were in first grade, and my friend Melanie Rosen got her *second* Cabbage Patch doll and I didn't even have one yet.

And like when Mandy was born, and Michael rang our doorbell, yelling, "Guess what, I have a baby sister!" And all I felt was, How come *he* gets one, when *I*'ve been wanting one for I don't know how long! I envied him so much, it took me a while before I could say "Congratulations" and act happy for him.

Well, it took Michael the whole way to school till he finally said, "Gee, Becky, that's great. Will you send me a postcard?"

Back in May, our class had done a unit on Washington and Oregon. So now during Social Studies Ms. Field made an announcement: "Class, you'll be interested to hear that Becky Suslow will be going to Portland, Oregon, to check it out for herself."

Kids said, "Wow," and "You're so lucky." It felt great, everybody envying me.

I had to wait two whole weeks, though. It seemed like forever. I thought July 1st wouldn't come for a few million years.

Finally it did!

My seat was in the front of the plane and by a window. When the plane lifted up off the ground that was the most thrilling moment in my whole, whole life.

The houses and streets got tiny. Then the plane curved around and the earth looked like it was tilting up, but it straightened out again when we flew over Manhattan. I saw the World Trade Center, the Empire State Building, all those skyscrapers; even Central Park, the East River, and the Hudson. Then everything got feathery gray, like inside an eiderdown quilt, because we were flying through clouds. And out again, above them, into the clear bright blue.

Now the clouds were under us! First they looked like a sky full of sheep. Then I started seeing different shapes in them. A dog's face with floppy ears. A rhinoceros. A castle with towers. A giant cow with wings.

The flight attendant kept bringing me stuff. *Ranger Rick* and *Cricket*. Striped peppermint candy they only give to people in first class—and to kids traveling alone. And she asked: Did I want crayons and a coloring book, or games, or anything?

"No, thank you." I had everything! Flying over cloud land, headed out to Portland to see Dad, what else could I possibly want?

After my cat, Whiskers, died, I drew a picture of her and lots of other cats flying around in heaven, having a fine time. I only did it to make myself feel better. I didn't really believe there was a place like that. But outside the airplane window it sure looked like it. And I hadn't had to die to get there. No, just the opposite. I felt the widest awake and most alive I'd ever felt in my life!

Suddenly Halloween

"Dad!"

He's so tall, I saw him right away. I ran down the ramp as if my sneakers had wings on them.

He swooped me up, brought my face close to his. "Boodle, you look beautiful!" We gave each other a big reunion kiss. He set me down. "And you've grown at least two inches since I last saw you."

"You look great, too, Dad."

He is really handsome. I don't think so just

because I'm his daughter. Other people think so, too. He has thick black hair and the darkest, velvety-sparkling brown eyes. He wore his faded old blue-and-brown plaid shirt. He once told me he'll wear it till it's in tatters because, of all the shirts he's got, it's my favorite.

"I'm so glad to see you!" We always say that right away. If I say it first, he answers, "Ditto, ditto, Becky-oh." If he says it first, I answer, "Ditto, ditto, Dad-oh!"

One time I asked him, "How come we love saying that so much?"

And he said, "Well, for me, it makes a kind of bridge back over all the time we couldn't be to-gether."

Hm. Yes, it made that kind of bridge for me, too.

"Dad, listen, I've got so many things to tell you—" About the plane, how great it was, and how the earth looked like a map, and shapes I saw in the clouds.

I talked and talked. The whole time we waited for my suitcase to come bumping down the chute and ride over to us on the luggage carousel. All the way to the parking lot, to his car, and all the way into Portland.

"Becky, honey, hold it a sec. See, we're about to cross a river, that's the Willamette. And see that very high mountain way over in the distance with snow on top? That's Mount Hood."

I looked and I kept on talking.

"Whoa, slow down," Dad said. "You're all jangly. Try and relax a little bit. There's no need to get everything said right this minute. We'll have lots and lots of time. And I've got things to tell you, too. How about letting me get a word in?"

"Okay, but Dad, listen, I was so thrilled when you sent me the tickets! Nobody in my whole class has ever been out here. I'm the first! And you know what, I thought today would never come, the time went slow as snails. I wanted it to hurry up. Now that I'm here I want it to slow down again."

I chatterboxed on till all of a sudden I ran out of steam.

"Flying can do that," Dad said. "The three-hour-time change does it, too. You don't realize how tired you are, because it's still light out. But if you were in Brooklyn, it would be dark and you'd be going to bed now."

Right, because in the middle of saying, "I'm not tired," I had to yawn, I just couldn't help it.

"We're here." Dad pulled into the driveway of a red house with white trim, an upstairs porch, a downstairs porch, and a pointed roof. "I hope you like it."

I opened the car door. But I couldn't get out, because this big white-and-brown dog came racing over, and he put his paws on my legs and started sniffing me.

Dad said, "Henry, stop it, get down."

A woman came down the front steps and over to my side of the car. "Henry, you behave yourself! Hi, Becky, I'm Rosellen. Welcome to Portland."

But I still couldn't get out because now Henry had his paws on my shoulders and was licking my cheek.

Rosellen scolded him, "That's no way to act. Get down."

He just went ahead and licked my other cheek.

I'm not that used to dogs. His breath was sweet, though, for a dog, and he didn't slobber. I petted him on the neck. I was thinking how nice his fur felt—when all of a sudden this little Halloween witch came running, yelling, "Henry, you get down!"

Henry did, quick as a flash.

She had a tall black cardboard hat on and a wide black cloak that floated in the wind. She pretended she was riding on a broomstick. She was really little. And she had makeup on: three black eyebrow-pencil lines across her forehead. Those were supposed to be wrinkles. And a lipstick frown drawn on in bright purple. Her real mouth smiled though, and she said, "Becky, you finally got here!"

Hey, I knew that voice . . .

Rosellen took her by the hand. "What are you doing in that outfit? Go on upstairs and change."

"Later. I want to be with Becky!"

"Now." Rosellen took her in the house. Henry trailed after them.

By then I'd figured out where I'd heard that voice before. And I felt like when the plane was landing, only even more so. *Thud*. Everything kind of spun around and my stomach bounced up and down. How come nobody'd said a word to me that *she*'d be here???

Dad got my suitcase out of the back. "Let's go inside."

"Wait, Dad. Was that Hope?"

"Right. How do you know her name?"

So then I told him how I'd gotten the wrong

number—only, it was the right one. I just didn't know at the time. And about that dumb Hope Who, Hope-you-go-soak-your-head routine.

Dad said, "She shouldn't fool around on the phone like that. Rosellen'll have a talk with her about it."

"Rosellen's her mother, right?"

"Yes."

"How come you didn't tell me?"

Dad's eyes get even darker when he feels bad about something. "It was hard to, on the phone. I was waiting for you to get here."

"But then when I got here, you still didn't tell me!"

"I know. I tried." He smiled. He put his arm around me. "You had so much to tell me, I couldn't get a word in."

"Dad, how come she has to be here just when I'm here?"

"It couldn't be helped. We didn't know, ourselves. She was supposed to spend this month in Tacoma, Washington. That's where her father and stepmother live."

"Yeah. Only she decided to get on her broomstick and come down here, just when I was coming."

"No, that's not what happened."

"What did happen?"

"Well, this morning her stepmom didn't feel well and had to go to the hospital. So her dad drove Hopie down here."

"What's wrong with her stepmom? I started to ask, but another yawn came over me.

"Hey, I thought you said you weren't tired!" Dad set my suitcase on the ground, so he could put both his arms around me. "Listen, Boodle, everything's all worked out. I have no outside work this whole week. I'll spend the whole time with you. And Rosellen's taking tomorrow off from her job, so she can take care of Hope, and you and I'll have your whole first day in Portland to ourselves. Doesn't that sound great?"

Soup Betrayal

Hope sat across from me during dinner. Her face was shiny from scrubbing the witch makeup off. She's got great big blue eyes, curly red hair, and a tiny freckle-speckled nose, the kind of looks that grown-ups think are "cute as a button." She acted like she thought she was pretty cute, too, smiling these sugar-sweet smiles at me, and saying she'd been waiting and waiting to meet me, and wasn't it lucky I came to visit just when *she* was here.

She wanted me to sleep in her room. She pestered, "Mom and Dan, please say she can!" This bothered me. So did the way she called my father Dan. I didn't like how that sounded. Dad told her I was used to sleeping in my own room.

"Becky needs her rest," said Rosellen. "So do you. You'll see Becky in the morning."

I loved the room they put me in. It had a sloping ceiling, because it was right under the roof, and the walls had rosebud wallpaper. It was very cozy, and easy to fall asleep in.

But I only slept for a couple of minutes. Then there was a big loud creak. Slowly the door started opening. Dim light shone in from the hall. Two shadowy shapes came in. One with a pointy hat on, the other with four legs. For about a second I didn't know where I was or who they were.

Till one put his paws on my bed, and the other said, "Can Henry come up?"

Henry did, before I even said Yes.

"Becky, were you sleeping?"

"Yes, I was."

"I'm sorry I woke you up."

"I'm sorry you did, too."

"Don't be mad, okay? I just couldn't wait till

morning. I have to tell you something. It's excit-
ing. And important. You'll really want to know
about it."

"What is it?"

"Why I wore my witch costume to say Hello
to you in, even though Mom told me not to. Same
reason I've got the hat on right now. It's a secret.
I haven't told it to anybody. But I'll tell it to you
if you want me to."

"Okay, go ahead."

"Well, the costume because it goes with the hat.
And the hat"—she whispered this part in my ear,
as if it was so secret that not even Henry should
hear it—"the hat can make things happen."

"It can? What kind of things?"

"Any things I want it to. If you don't believe
it, I can prove it to you. Remember when you first
got here and how Henry jumped up on you? And
my mom and your dad said, 'Henry, get down,'
and he wouldn't? But when *I* told him to, he did?
The hat made it happen, that's why."

"You woke me up to tell me *that*? See him
sitting on my stomach? Watch, I'll make him move
over. Without a witch's hat."

And I said, "Henry, please move over." And
he did. "See? He moved over, just like that."

"That's nothing, I've got a bigger proof. Want to hear it?"

"Sure."

"Okay, but it's even more secret: Ruthie, she's my stepmom, will have a baby soon. And the hat is making it be a girl."

I thought, Oh wow. And I told her, "A hat can't do that! Nobody can, not even the greatest doctors in the world."

"This hat can. You'll see. It's definite. I already picked out a name for her. My dad and Ruthie asked me to. Want to know what I picked? Penelope. Isn't that pretty?" Hope tugged at a curl near her ear, and stuck it in her mouth.

I asked her, "How old are you, anyway?"

"Six and one month."

I tried to remember if I thought up really dumb things like that when I was her age. No. I already knew about babies. And that nobody has a say about what sex they are. Or else people could just place their orders for whichever they want, like for hamburgers, medium or rare.

"I'll call her Nelopie, for short. I like how that rhymes with Hopie, don't you?"

"Yes. Now would you let me sleep? And Henry, would you get down?"

He did.

"See? He did it again, no hat."

Hope said, "That's because he likes you."

"I like him, too. Now can I go back to sleep?"

"Wait. Aren't you going to ask me what I wished on the hat when you came?"

"Okay, what did you wish?"

"That's the most secret part. I can't tell you, or it won't come true."

"So why did you bring it up? Just to get me curious?"

She sucked on the curl some more. "I'd tell you, I really would, except I can't, because I want it to come true so much! But I'll let *you* make a wish. Here, put the hat on. Now first, you tap on it with your pinkie: one time, two times, three times. Go on, do it."

So I went, *tap, tap, tap*.

"Now wish."

"Okay." I gave her back the hat.

So then she asked, "What did you wish?"

"That you'd go out and let me sleep!"

She laughed. "You weren't supposed to tell! But okay, it's coming true. 'Night, Becky, sleep tight."

Hope and Henry went out. I fell back asleep.

Not for long, though. There she was again!

"Becky, I forgot to tell you something you'll really love. Wait till you hear what it is!"

I turned away, to the wall.

"Sorry I woke you up again, but you'll be glad, I promise." Then she asked, "What's your favorite food in the whole world?"

"Worms on toast. Leave me alone."

"I will, soon as you tell me your real favorite food."

"Peanut-butter and pickle sandwiches."

"No, I mean *really*."

"Those really are."

"What else?"

"Peach ice cream. Anchovies."

"What else? Think!"

"I can't, I'm too tired. Why do you want to know?"

"Oh, I just thought it would be something else, that's all," she said in mysterious way.

So I asked, "Something else like what?"

"*You* know. First onions have to sizzle. Then you put a bone in, then a bunch of other stuff. Midnight Soup."

I sat up. I was wide awake now. "How come *you* know about it?"

"Your father taught it to me. Want to hear all the stuff we put in? Parsley, peas—"

"No, just get out of here!" I threw myself back down flat and stuck the pillow over my head.

She started to go out. At the door she said, "And guess what, we put some in the freezer. So you can have some tomorrow. Aren't you glad?"

Thank You, Hat

A smell woke me up that I loved. Oil paints.
When I was little, as soon as that smell reached
my nose, I'd jump out of bed and go see what
Dad was painting.

I started to go downstairs.

Dad's easel was in the living room, by the window. He stood in front of it, facing away from
the stairs. But he heard me coming and said,
"Happy first morning in Portland!"

Just then I remembered the last thing Hope had

told me, and I stood still. Like my feet got glued to the stair.

Dad turned around. "Hey, Boodle, come tell me what's wrong."

I unglued my feet and went down. I never had trouble telling things to Dad before. But now I couldn't think of any words to tell him how I felt.

I went up to the easel.

He said, "I just started on this painting. There's not too much there yet."

Right. I thought of the paintings he used to do back when he still lived in Brooklyn with us. Lots of them were of things he saw looking out our windows: storefronts, cars, a fire hydrant, the mailbox on our corner. I liked those paintings a lot.

This new one only had a few thick white brushstrokes. I couldn't tell what it was going to be. I couldn't think of anything to say.

He said, "What's the Becky-Boo face for? Would you hold it just like that for a moment?"

He grabbed a sketch pad and drew me. With a few charcoal strokes. Just my face. "Okay, now tell me, what's bothering you? Is it Hope? That she's here with us?"

"It isn't only that."

"What else?" He held out his arms.

I couldn't say. And I couldn't go into his arms.

"Uh oh, trouble. How can we solve it? Would it help if I start breakfast?"

We went into the kitchen. He opened the refrigerator, took out milk and juice.

I opened the freezer. There. It stared me in the face, a big container with a label on it—MIDNITE SOUP. I took it out. Dad started squeezing oranges. I put it on the counter right in front of him.

"Oh, so that's it." He stuck it back in the freezer and squeezed more juice. He wrinkled his forehead, like he does when he's thinking about something.

He handed me my juice. He sat down next to me. "Okay, here's what happened. One night, I couldn't sleep. So I came down to do my usual, *you* know, make soup. Well, Hope was staying here—"

"It sounds like she stays here all the time."

"No, part of the time she stays in Tacoma. Anyway, she couldn't sleep either. She was homesick for her dad. She came downstairs and she wanted to help. So I let her. You would have, too. How about eating some of this cereal?"

Wheat Chex. I didn't want any.

Dad said, "I guess you're mad at me."

I said, "Couldn't you have cooked something else with her? Like stew, or I don't know what?"

"Well, maybe I should have. But look at it this way: you and I are so special to each other, we can afford to let somebody share in something we like to do—"

"*We* didn't. *You* let her."

"That's true." He took my face between his hands. "And I'm sorry it makes you feel bad. But it doesn't take away from how I feel about you."

He looked me straight in the eyes. When somebody does that, and you try to look straight back, especially if he's got velvety-sparkly eyes that show you exactly how he's feeling, after a while you start to smile, you can't help it. And then you both start laughing, no matter what.

Dad kissed me on my forehead, nose, cheeks, and chin. "This is how I feel about you. Is that understood?"

"Yes."

"So, have we made up?"

"Yes." And I told him how I felt about her. "Dad, Hope is so babyish! You know what she thinks? That her hat is magic and can make things

happen. You want to hear the dumbest thing? She thinks it'll make her stepmom's baby come out a girl."

Dad smiled. "Yes, that's pretty silly. But she's right about one thing." And he told me there's a test that shows what sex a baby is while it's still inside the mother. He said to ask Mom when I get home, that she'd explain it. "Anyway, Hope's stepmom, Ruth, had the test, and the baby'll be a girl. There's a problem, though. Ruthie's in labor. You know what that is?"

"Sure. The baby's starting to come out."

"Right, that's it. You see, the baby's not due for another six weeks. So it's kind of an emergency. That's why Hope's father brought her down here to stay with us."

And Henry, too. He came down the stairs, *whoof, whoofing,* like he was saying good morning.

Dad put some Kibbles 'n Bits in his bowl.

Next, *whoosssh,* Hope slid down the banister in her spaceship pajamas with the hat on. She landed on her behind. It made a pretty loud bang. But she just picked herself up and came in as if it was nothing, and asked, "Where are we going today?"

Dad said, "You and your mom are going some-place today, remember?"

"Why can't all of us go together?"

"Because it's Becky's first day here, and she and I haven't seen each other in a long time." Dad sounded like he'd already explained this to her a few times.

"Where will you and Becky go?"

Dad said, "We haven't decided yet."

I said, "How about the Talking Tree?" He'd sent me a postcard of it. Ms. Field put it on the class bulletin board when we did the unit on the Northwest.

Hope went, "Goodie, yeah, the Talking Tree," like it hadn't sunk in that only Dad and I were going.

Then Rosellen came down. I could see her from where I sat. She wore a long robe that made folds around her. It was the color of a forest. It was just a bathrobe, but it looked more like an evening gown on her. Her hair is reddish-brown. The night before she'd worn it pinned up. Now it hung down, all loose and wavy. When she went past the little window in back of the staircase, the sun shone through and lit up golden patches in her hair. Rosellen's beautiful. I couldn't help feeling a little bad. Dad's face got all happy when he saw her coming.

She sat down next to Hope. She leaned back in her chair, stretched her arms up over her head. "Mm, it feels delicious, not having to rush off to work for a change."

But when she'd had her juice and was buttering her toast, the phone rang. It was her boss at the museum where she works.

Hope made an I-know-something-you-don't-know face and tapped on her stupid hat.

Rosellen hung up. "Wouldn't you know? They need me to come in after all."

"Goodie!" Hope jumped up and down. "Thank you, Hat, you did it!"

"You're glad I have to go to work? That's not too nice of you."

"I'm not glad you have to go to work, Mom. I'm just glad because that way I get to go with Becky and Dan, hooray!"

"Not so fast," said Rosellen. "I promised Dan that he and Becky'd have this day alone, just the two of them. I'll ask the de Siricos if you can stay there today." They're good friends of hers and Dad's in the neighborhood. Rosellen called them.

Hope didn't want to stay with them. She tapped on the hat some more.

The de Siricos were going someplace, so Hope couldn't go over there. Rosellen called up some other friends. She went down her list of baby-sitters. Every time she dialed the phone, Hope tapped on the hat. And either the people weren't at home or they said, Sorry, they couldn't.

"Tell you what, Hopie, if you behave yourself, I'll take you with me to work, there're lots of interesting things to do there—"

"No, I'll act awful, I'll be a brat!" Hope hugged the hat to her chest and tapped on it with both her pinkies.

Rosellen looked up at the ceiling like she didn't know what to do next.

Dad sent me a look of, Sorry, Becky, and said, "It's okay, she'll come with us."

Hope jumped up and down like a yo-yo. "Thank you a million trillion times," she told the hat, and gave it a big smoochy kiss.

Elephant Language and Tree Talk

Henry came, too. *He* stayed in the back of the car and didn't bother anybody.

Dad's car is an old Pontiac with room for three in front. Guess who sat herself smack in the middle, and said, "You sit by the window, Becky, so you can see everything," like she was doing me a big favor.

"No, thanks, I'll sit next to my father. Move over."

She wouldn't budge. Dad had to lift her up and

move her over. "But then *I* get to sit in the middle going home, okay?"

I said, "Not okay."

Dad tried to reason with her. "Hope, think, if you hadn't seen your father in a very long time, wouldn't you want to sit next to him? Try putting yourself in Becky's shoes—"

"You mean, her sneakers; all *right*!"

I was wearing the ones Grandma Sonia gave me; they look like they have jewels on them. Hope dived down to the floor of the car and started untying the laces.

I said, "Hey, cut that out!"

"I'm just doing what your father said, putting myself in your sneakers." *Giggle, giggle.* "I love your sneakers, they're so pretty." And she wouldn't quit.

Till Dad said, "Look, Hope, we're coming to your old neighborhood."

That made her sit up. "See that house with the swing on the porch? That used to be our house. And guess who painted it blue! Dan, your dad, and he let me paint the gingerbread. Didn't I do a good job?"

"Gingerbread? On a house? What are you talking about?"

"That lacy-looking white trim, that's what it's called, isn't it, Dan?" She sounded thrilled to pieces that she knew something I didn't know.

Pretty soon we came to a bridge, and I asked, "Are we crossing the Willamette River?"

"It's not Willamette!" She bounced up and down, she was so delighted that I'd said it wrong. "People not from here always say it that way, but it's Willamette! Isn't that right, Dan?"

"Right," said my father, "but, Hope, take it easy, would you?"

Then I saw that mountain with the snow on top that we'd seen on the ride from the airport, and I said, "There's Mount Hood again."

Dad said, "It's my favorite mountain of all the mountains I was ever on."

Hope wanted us to go there, but Dad said it was too far. "Besides, today we're showing Becky Portland."

We saw the Television Center Tower, the Portland Building with a big statue of Portlandia on it, and the Pacwest Center, all silvery on the outside. We took a walk around the port and saw the ships. We ate lunch in Chinatown.

Then we went to the zoo. It's famous for its great big herd of elephants. And they're not cooped

up in a small, smelly place like in the zoo at home.
They have lots of room to roam around in. They
were in the jungly part, so far away from the moat,
we almost couldn't see them.

Hope said, "Want me to call them? I know
how."

"Go ahead. Tell them to hurry up."

"All right, I will!" And she let out a noise like
you never heard in your life. It was a *shriek-yell-
blast* on a trumpet all rolled into one, so loud
people couldn't believe it. A baby in a stroller
started crying. A bunch of kids near us started
imitating it.

"The elephants will be right over," said Hope.
"I called them in elephant language. I learned it
from a movie on TV, about this man who knows
animal languages, and he called the elephants just
like that and about a hundred of them came."

"So why aren't these coming?" I asked.

"They will. They're just taking their time."

We waited around. Nothing happened.

"Hey, Elephant Girl, when are they coming?"
teased a boy about my age.

Hope got embarrassed. "I don't know why it
didn't work."

"Do it again!" The kids egged her on.

But Dad said, "No." He took her by the hand. "Come on, let's see some other animals."

After the zoo we went to the World Forestry Center. Hope was in a hurry to see the Talking Tree.

"There's the bathroom. Hope, do you need to go?" Dad asked.

"No. I'm old enough to know myself when I have to go."

So we went and saw the tree. It's supposed to be a Douglas fir. It looks 100 percent real. There's even a squirrel, an owl, and some little birds on its branches. You'd never guess that it's made of fiberglass.

The trunk is really roomy, and you can go inside.

Dad, Hope, and I, a boy around twelve, a girl around five, and their mother went inside. The boy pushed the button that starts it talking. First there was only a crackling sound, like it was clearing its throat. I couldn't wait to hear what it would say.

"I have to go to the bathroom!"

A hush. Everyone kept quiet. Nobody wanted to be the first to laugh or anything.

"Mommy, did you hear that?" said the little

girl, "the tree has to go to the bathroom!" So then the boy broke up laughing. Their mother tried not to, but she had to laugh, too.

Meantime the tree, I mean, the recording in it, was saying, "Welcome to the World Forestry Center . . ."

"We'll meet you outside," Dad said in my ear and rushed Hope out of there.

"I'm a typical Douglas fir tree," said the recording. "I'm sixty feet tall. My trunk is six feet across at the base. And I need two hundred gallons of water a day."

"No wonder," said the boy. That got me laughing, too, even though I felt kind of sorry for Hope.

They waited near the exit. Her face was red as ketchup. The elephants not obeying her call was nothing compared to what happened in the Talking Tree. She was mortified. She stared at her feet. She was really down in the dumps, so I said, "Hey, don't feel so bad, it can happen to anybody."

On the drive back she perked up and pestered about sitting in the middle, till Dad had had it up to his eyeballs.

He sent me a look that said, Please try not to mind, and he gave in. "Oh, all right. Becky'll be a good sport about it."

I hate that "be a good sport" stuff. It means

that something unfair's about to happen and you're not supposed to do anything or say anything to stop it.

Hope climbed over me and plonked herself in the middle.

"You're very quiet, Becky-oh," Dad said after awhile.

After another while, we came to the bridge, and he said, "Penny for your thoughts."

Well, here's what I was thinking: that it really, really bothered me that Hope sat in the middle. It spoiled the whole ride. Also, about what Dad said when I first got here, how he and I like to make bridges across the time we have to be apart. Well, with Hope sitting between us, it was more like a drawbridge when it's up, and you're stuck, you can't get across it. And here's another thing I thought: she's the brattiest kid I ever met. He never should have let her sit there.

Dad said, "Well? Aren't you going to tell me?"

"No. You wouldn't want to hear."

"I want to hear anything you have to say. You and I don't keep secrets from each other. Do we, Becky?"

I didn't answer. I kept quiet the whole rest of the way.

Mothball in the Mints

It was late. I was supposed to be in bed. But I'd bought a bunch of postcards: two of downtown Portland, for Melanie and Kyra; one of ships in the port, for Mrs. Galloway; one of a tiger in the zoo, for Michael; and the prettiest of all—of meadows and hills and Mount Hood in the distance—for Mom. I wanted to get started writing them.

First I wrote to Kyra, then to Melanie. About

the plane, about the places I'd seen so far, and that Portland was great. "Except," I wrote to Kyra, "there's a pretty big fly in the ointment."

One time last spring, in Language Arts, our class was supposed to think up new ways of saying that. Like, there's a lump in the Jell-O. Or, there's a grease spot on the dress. The ones that Jason Abeloff made up were so gross, Ms. Field wouldn't let him write on the board: a rat's tail in the tuna salad. A blood-sucking leech in the bathtub.

Anyway, on the card to Melanie, I wrote, "Portland's great, except there's a mothball in the mints." And I started getting prickles on the back of my neck, the way you do when someone's watching.

Someone was. "What do you mean, 'a mothball in the mints'?"

I wheeled around. "None of your business!"

"Aren't you surprised I can read script? Don't you think that's pretty good for somebody my age?"

"Don't brag. You're not supposed to read private things people write to their friends."

She put her finger in her mouth and wheedled, "Come on, Becky, what's 'a mothball in the mints'?"

"Same thing as 'a fly in the ointment.' It's a saying."

"Oh." She thought about it and stopped looking so pleased with herself. "I'm the fly, right? I'm the mothball." Her chin started to quiver. "You know what? You hurt my feelings."

"That can happen when you stick your nose where it doesn't belong."

"You think I'm a baby."

I said, "Well, sometimes you act like one."

"I can't help it." She scrunched up her face the way little kids do before they start to cry. "I'm scared."

"What of?"

"That my hat's not working anymore."

"What makes you think that?"

"Well, remember I told you I made a wish on it when you first came?"

"Yes, I remember. What was it?"

"I'm still not telling. But the hat's not making it come true." She sniffled. "So now I'm scared it won't make the other thing come true, either."

"You mean about Nelopie?"

"Right. And Ruthie's sick, that scares me, too. And I miss my dad." She let out a big sob.

I sat her down on my bed and tried to make her feel better.

After a while she did. She asked, "Can I look through your glasses?"

"You wouldn't like it. No one but me can see straight with them on. I never let anybody."

"Please, please, let me."

"No, but I'll tell you something funny. When I was your age, I used to sleep with my glasses on, so I could see my dreams better."

So then she wanted to look through them even more, and I let her. "Everything's blurry," she said.

"Give 'em back. And I'll let you see something not blurry." I opened my locket and showed her the pictures in it of Mom and Whiskers.

Somebody knocked at the door.

"Knock, that's what you're supposed to do, instead of come barging in." And I thought, Please, let it be Dad. He'd said good night to me and all, but still, I really wanted to see him. And I said, "Come in."

It was Rosellen. She was looking for Hope. "So this is where you're hiding out. I came to tuck you in and you weren't in your bed. Come on, time to go to sleep. You, too, Becky, aren't you tired?"

I said, "Sort of."

Rosellen asked, "Want me to tuck you in?"

"No, thank you." I really meant Yes. But I didn't know her that well, and I didn't want to sound like a baby.

After they went out I had this big, empty, sad feeling inside. I shuffled the three other postcards. I took the one I'd bought for Mom, of the meadow with flowers, of hilly orchards in bloom, and, way in the distance, the peak of Mount Hood. And I thought about Mom, and I missed her so much that I couldn't write it.

I thought, Dad thinks he knows me pretty well. Why doesn't he know how I'm feeling right now? Why doesn't he come up? I took the tiger card. I thought about how Michael's father made Michael sweep the floor that day, and how Michael got so mad at him. I took my pen and I doodled a knot in the tiger's tail, thinking, Michael's right, fathers can be really unfair. I got mad at mine all over again for letting Hope sit next to him. And for not telling me about her in the first place.

The knot in the tiger's tail got thick and blotchy. It loused up the card.

I got into bed but couldn't fall asleep. I lay there and made up a meadow behind my eyelids, a lot like the one on the postcard for Mom. I put me,

Mom, and Dad in the middle of it, on a blanket with a picnic basket.

When I was little I could make up wonderful pictures like that, and I'd fall asleep and dream them.

Now, instead of getting drowsy, I got wider awake. And I thought, If the three of us had a picnic like that, what about Hope? Well, she could be with her dad and stepmom. But then, what about Rosellen? And what about Mom's friend Pete? How would they feel? So I made up another nice place, a beach with high waves, and I put them on it. But they didn't want to be there. The whole thing didn't work and I couldn't get to sleep.

My friend Kyra thinks that if you concentrate with all your might you can send someone a mental message. Especially if the person is in the same house. I tried. I squeezed my eyes shut, I even held my breath. *Dad, come on up here!*

No good. It wasn't reaching him.

So finally I decided, Okay, then I'll go down. And I started to go down the stairs—just when he was starting to come up!

We met in the middle. He said, "I was just going to check if you needed anything."

"Like what, for instance?"

"Like a hug, for instance. I know *I* could use one."

"I could use one, too."

So then we put our arms around each other and went upstairs like that. He tucked me in. " 'Night, Boodle."

" 'Night, Dad."

And I slept just fine.

Next day, my third day in Portland, started better. Rosellen didn't go to work. She took care of Hope.

Dad and I went sight-seeing to the greatest place! The Columbia River Gorge, which was truly gorgeous, and had waterfalls—six of them! When I'd never even seen *one* waterfall in my whole life before.

It was very peaceful in the car with just the two of us. And he told me the whole thing about what was happening with Hope's stepmom and the baby. "It's a big worry. But you're old enough to understand. She's still in labor. The doctor hoped it would stop. If the baby's born now, she'll be tiny. She'll be a preemie."

"Will they put her in an incubator?"

"Yes."

My mom and I've had lots of talks about babies getting born. They're supposed to stay inside the mother for nine months. Then they're in good shape when they come out and can breathe on their own, and cry, and start sucking milk. But when they're preemies, they don't know how to do those things yet. They have a hard time, and it's not certain that they'll be okay.

Dad and I talked about that. And about Hope feeling scared, even though she didn't know exactly what was happening. It was very rough on her. I made up my mind I'd be nice to her, no matter how bratty she got.

Fry a Hen!

That night was the Fourth of July fireworks, and I'd been looking forward to them the whole day.

We went early and got a good spot. Even so, Hope said, "I can't see, I can't see," and made Dad put her on his shoulders. She acted pretty bratty. I tried not to let it bother me.

They had more kinds of fireworks than I'd ever seen. Rosellen knew what they were called: silver streaks, space dazzlers, weeping willows. That's what they looked like, too.

"Here comes a diamond cloud," Rosellen said when Hope started whining, "Mom, my stomach hurts!"

"Come sit on my lap." Rosellen rubbed Hope's stomach for a while. "Now watch this green one going up, it'll be a palm tree."

It shot way up high.

"My stomach really hurts," Hope went on, really loud.

Dad said, "Lie down. That'll help."

"Then I won't be able to see!"

"Hopie, don't whine. Take deep breaths and you'll feel better," said Rosellen. "Look, there goes another space dazzler."

"I feel worse, I want to go home!"

Dad said in a tight voice, "Rosellen, don't let her spoil this whole evening for everyone."

Rosellen said, "I'm trying. Now, Hopie—"

A red flower-shower rocket, the best kind, was showering down through the sky. Hope made a horrible noise in her throat.

I said, "You're making yourself throw up."

"I am not! I can't help it, I feel sick!"

Dad said, "Oh boy. Why did you let her eat all those Fritos?"

"Why did *you*?" Rosellen said back. "You could have stopped her, too."

Their voices sounded like they were going to have a fight about it. But then Rosellen stood up and said to my father, "You and Becky stay. Come on, Hopie, we'll wait in the car."

"No." Dad stood up, too. "If she's really sick, we'd better get her home."

And the fireworks weren't even half over!

On the way to the parking lot Hope said to me, "I bet you don't believe that I'm really sick." She didn't sound it, either.

"You're right, I don't. I think you're a brat and you spoil everything," I said, and—wouldn't you know?—just that moment she bent over and threw up all over the ground.

She lay on Rosellen's lap for most of the drive back. By the time we turned into Dad's street she was sitting up and said, "Guess what, I'm better."

When we were almost at the house, Henry barked and yowled like crazy, and before we knew it he'd squeezed out through a window.

A blue Chevrolet with a dented fender was parked in front of the house. A man got out. Henry jumped all over him.

As soon as Dad stopped the car, Hope jumped

out, too, and ran over to him. He lifted her up and kissed her all over her face and hair. He was her dad, Mr. Levy.

He was pudgy, with a bald spot, not that good-looking, but he looked good to me. Because I thought maybe, just maybe, he'd come to take Hope back to Tacoma, and I'd be rid of her.

We all went in the house and he told the big news: "Penelope was born today, at a quarter past noon. She weighs three pounds and four ounces, she's doing fine in her incubator. She'll get bigger soon. And Ruthie's doing fine, too."

"Yippee, that's wonderful, when can I see Nelopie?" said Hope.

Mr. Levy took her on his lap. "Soon."

"When? Tomorrow?"

"Not that soon."

"How come? Aren't you taking me back with you?"

"I wish I could, sweetie." He tried to explain that on account of his job and having to rush back and forth to the hospital, he wouldn't have enough time to take care of her. "You're better off staying here a little while longer with your mom and Dan and Becky."

"No, I want to go with you! I'm not better off

here. Becky says I'm a brat and I spoil everything."
She hid her face in his shirt.

Rosellen sent Dad a long look. I didn't know
her that well, so I wasn't sure, but I thought she
probably blamed him for the awful thing I'd said
to Hope. I felt terrible.

Dad came over to me, put his hand on my
shoulder. "Becky, did you really say that?"

I nodded. I'd have liked to crawl into a hole.

"Well," said Dad to the others, "I'm sure Becky
didn't mean it. It was only because the fireworks
were so great, and Hope getting a stomach-ache
meant we had to leave. Right, Becky?"

"I guess so."

But Hope was crying "Daddy, I want to see
Nelopie and Ruthie" so loud, nobody even
heard me.

Next morning when I came downstairs Dad
told me that things were not so good with Nelopie.
She had some kind of infection. That often happens with preemies. They were giving her medi-
cine for it, and she might get better. The way he
said it, it sounded like she might not, too. My
teeth started chattering. I got scared. It sounded
like Nelopie might not pull through.

So then I felt like a horrible person, for being

so mean to Hope. I didn't know how I could face her, or Rosellen, either. "Where are they, anyway?" I asked.

"Outside. Hope's father just left."

Hope and Rosellen stood in the driveway. Rosellen held on to Henry's collar so he wouldn't chase after the blue Chevrolet. Hope waved till it was out of sight.

Then they came around the side of the house into the backyard. I could see them out the kitchen window. Rosellen sat down in the tire swing. Hope got into her lap, and they swung back and forth.

After a while they came in. Rosellen said, "I'd better start those chickens soon, to bring to the de Siricos." The de Siricos were having a Fourth of July picnic that afternoon and we were invited. "Hopie, want to help? You can dip the pieces in the breading."

"No." Hope flopped down on the couch and sucked on the ends of her hair.

I went over to her. "I'm sorry I said those things. Make up with me?" I held out my hand.

She knocked it away.

"I'll play with you. Anything you want. How about Go Fish?"

"Uh uh, no!" She rolled herself into a ball and cried.

Rosellen sighed, sat down on the couch, put Hope's head in her lap, and stroked her hair.

Dad said, "Stay right there. Don't worry about the chickens. I'll start on them. Becky, you give me a hand."

We went to the kitchen. He took out the chicken pieces, flour, eggs, and breadcrumbs. "Now let's see, which do you dip it in first?"

"Flour. Then egg. Then crumbs. At least, that's how Grandma Sonia does it."

We did it that way, too. We let the oil get good and hot in the pan. Then we put the pieces in, carefully, so we wouldn't get spattered.

After awhile Rosellen and Hope came in. Hope had tear streaks down her cheeks, but she wasn't crying anymore. Rosellen said, "Thanks, you guys. We'll take over now."

She sounded nice. Like, if she'd been mad at me before, she wasn't anymore.

The chicken pieces got crisp and golden. They made a good smell, just like in my grandma's kitchen, and I said, "Hey, Hopie, want to hear a song my grandmother made up?"

Hope was still mad at me. "No."

"It's about frying chickens. You'll like it."

"Okay."

So I sang it. It's short; it only has two lines: " 'If at first you don't succeed, / Fry, fry a hen!' " I gave it a lot of expression, so she'd get the joke.

Hope stayed poker-faced. "That's silly. That's not how it goes!"

But Rosellen smiled, like she appreciated it, and sent me a look of, Thanks for trying.

So I tried real hard, the whole weekend long.

There was another girl just my age, Sharon Lucas, at the de Siricos' picnic. She and I had fun playing Ping-Pong, darts, and horseshoes. We could have had a lot more fun if Hope hadn't stuck to us like glue. But I let her. Finally, when we were playing "Chopsticks" on the de Siricos' piano and Hope kept going *plim, plim, plim* on the black keys, Sharon got fed up and went to hang out with a bunch of older kids.

When we got back from the picnic, Mr. Levy called and said that Nelopie had gained two ounces. The next day, Saturday, it rained all day. We went to a shopping mall and bought magnetized Pick-up-Stix. We played a few games, but Hope wasn't too good at it, so I looked the other way a couple of times and let her win.

Then we gave Henry a bath. We didn't do much else. I guess what we were really doing was waiting for news about Nelopie. But Mr. Levy didn't call. So finally Rosellen called the hospital in Tacoma, and she and Hope spoke to Ruth.

Sunday, Mr. Levy called, first thing, and said things looked good. Nelopie didn't have the infection anymore. So we didn't have to hang around the phone all day. We all went to a beach Rosellen knew on the Columbia River. The water was pretty cold, but we went in anyway. Hope only knew how to dog-paddle. I got her to put her face in and I tried to teach her the crawl.

Sunday night she did her trick again, of coming into my room, but I don't know when. I didn't even know she was there till I turned over in my sleep. There she lay, right next to me! I sat up. "What are you doing in here?"

"Oh good, you're awake, I've been waiting and waiting! I have to tell you stuff."

I groaned. "Listen, I want to be rested up for tomorrow, it's my last day in Portland—"

"I know. And I thought, What if I don't get a chance to talk to you?"

"How about in the morning?"

"No, I have to ask you something. It's a secret, you're the only person I can ask."

That got me curious, and I said, "Go ahead."

"When you first heard about my mom, did you mind? Did you think you'd hate her?"

"Not exactly."

"What, then?"

"I thought I might not like her. And that she might not like me, either."

"Good. I'm so, so glad!"

"How come?"

"Because I felt like that, too, about your dad, when he and my mom first met each other. After a while I started liking him. Now I like him a real lot. You'll like my mom, too, she's nice."

"I know. I already do."

"There's something else, Becky. About my hat. You think I'm dumb that I believe in it, don't you? Well, I don't believe in it that much anymore."

"Why not? Your stepmom's baby came out a girl, just like you wished."

"I know. But Mom said my hat didn't make it happen."

"What about the wish you made when I first got here?"

Hope said, "I just about gave up on that." She reached for the hat. It was on the night table. She tapped on it with her pinkie.

"What did you wish? Come on, tell me."

"I can't, 'cause I still want it to come true, even more than before."

"Come on, Hopie. Please?"

"Uh uh."

By then I wanted to know so badly, I begged, I didn't care if I whined. "Tell me, tell me, please, please, please. I'll do anything. I'll be your friend—"

"You will?" She started giggling happily and hugged and kissed the hat. "Okay, then how about going downstairs right now and making Midnight Soup, sweet-and-sour style? We can use maple syrup for sweet and pickle juice for sour."

"Yuk. Forget it!"

"You said you'd do anything."

"But not that. Let me sleep now, please!"

But she wouldn't. I got really tired. Finally I told her, "Get out of here, leave me alone."

So she went.

"Hey, you forgot the hat," I called. But she was already out the door.

Hanukkah in July

Next thing I thought, Oh no, she's back! I turned to the wall and I pretended to snore.

"Becky, honey, wake up." It was Dad! "Get dressed. Wear your heavy jeans and a sweater. And bring your sweatshirt, too." He ducked under the bed, came up with my regular sneakers. "Put these on, hurry up."

"What time is it? Where are we going?

"Shh, Rosellen and Hope are still sleeping. It's

a quarter to seven. We're going someplace great."
He went downstairs to start breakfast.

I never put my clothes on that fast before in
my life. I went down the banister Hope-style. Then
I was too excited to eat breakfast, so Dad put an
orange and a sesame roll in a bag for me to have
in the car.

Henry came out to the driveway with us. Dad
scratched him on the head. "Sorry, fella, you're
staying home."

Henry looked sad. I kissed him on his smooth
cheek. "So long, see you later."

We drove and drove a long, long way, through
hilly farm country. There were very few houses.
We went past fields of tall grass, just starting to
turn into hay. Past orchards with little apples and
pears already on the trees. We stopped at a fruit
stand and bought plums and cherries.

We drove some more. The hills got higher and
pretty soon, straight ahead, there was a white peak.
I said, "Look, Dad, your favorite mountain!"

"Yeah. Isn't it something?"

Then we came into woods, and all we saw for
a long time were trees, trees, trees—mostly firs.
The sun shone through them and made patterns
of light and dark on the ground. The road curved

around and started to climb. My ears closed up, then they popped. We were driving up, up, up. And we couldn't see the peak anymore. I asked, "Where's Mount Hood?"

"This is it. We're going up it!"

The trees got fewer. Soon there weren't any. Suddenly the peak appeared, right before our eyes. And near it we could see people skiing down a slope.

We came to a big building made of dark brown logs. It was a lodge.

Dad parked and we left our stuff in the car.

There were trails leading in all directions. We followed one that led through meadows filled with yellow, white, red, blue, and purple mountain flowers. We came to a rock with a smooth hollowed-out place that looked like an armchair for two people. We sat there together. Above us was the snow peak meeting the sky. Below were the dark green woods, and all around us were flower meadows like the one we came through.

I was so happy. I said, "I never thought there could be any place this beautiful in the whole world."

"Me, too," said Dad. He looked and looked. "I'm filling up my eyes with it."

I said, "That's what I'm doing, too."

Soon we were starving. "From the mountain air," said Dad. "Come on." We went back to the lodge and ate lunch there.

After lunch Dad made us rest awhile in big wooden chairs on the veranda. After that we got our sweatshirts from the car and followed another trail, a steep one, up to the top of the mountain.

"Now we have a choice," said Dad. "Do we go farther up and watch the skiers from up close? Or do we take a swim?"

How? The ski slope looked miles away. And I didn't see a lake to swim in anywhere; besides, I hadn't brought my bathing suit, and it was cold. I asked him, "Are you kidding?"

He laughed. "Just stick with me."

We went a little farther up the trail and came to a ski chair lift. "How about it? Are you game?"

I said, "Sure."

He put up the hood of my sweatshirt and tied it under my chin. "Okay, hop on."

The seat swung high off the ground. Wind whistled around my face as I sailed up and up through the air. But Dad was right behind me, so instead of feeling scared I loved it.

The ski lift stopped at the top of the ski run.

We watched the skiers. It looked like fun. And we talked about how, next time I came to Portland, I'd stay longer, maybe long enough to spend a couple of days up here and learn to ski.

Then we went back down to the lodge. Dad said, "Guess what, I brought our bathing suits. They're in the car."

We went and got them. I still didn't see any lake. But right behind the lodge there was a wonderful pool. And it was heated, so the water was nice and warm.

We floated on our backs and gazed up at the peak glistening in the sky. It was so beautiful, and the water felt so terrific, and the sun shone down so warm!

I said, "I love it here. This is the best part of my whole visit."

Dad said, "I think this is the only place in the whole country where people can swim and ski in July."

That reminded me of something. "Dad, remember when I called you up and you wouldn't tell me when I could come, and I said, How about when Hanukkah's in July?"

"Mm hm, I remember."

"Well, now I feel like it really is. And I'm not being sarcastic."

He said, "I know you're not."

It was getting late. We changed back into our clothes. Dad said, "We ought to start back." First, though, we went to the souvenir shop. And I saw something I really liked: a see-through paperweight shaped like a globe, except it had a flat bottom, so it could stand. Inside was a tiny mountain that looked like Mount Hood and, near the top, a teensy dark brown house that looked like the lodge. On the bottom was white stuff. When you shook it, it floated up and whirled around and came down like a snowstorm. It cost $3.95.

I still had $3.00 left from the money Mom had given me. Dad gave me 95 cents and I bought it for myself.

On the way back I wondered where Hope and Rosellen had gone today. Someplace good, I hoped. Or Hope would make a big fuss when she found out where Dad and I'd been.

It was dark when we got back to the house. I got ready for Henry to come dashing to the car and jump up on me. No Henry.

Only Rosellen came out. "Did you two have a great day?"

"The greatest. Excuse me." I rushed past her into the house. I needed to go to the bathroom very badly. I kind of expected Hope to bang on the door and be all eager to see me. Well, she didn't. So when I came out, I peeked into her room, thinking maybe she was already asleep. Nobody in there.

So then I thought maybe she'd decided to go to sleep in my bed and I went into my room. Nobody in there either. Her hat was still on my night table where she'd left it the night before. Seeing it standing there made me feel kind of crummy.

I went across the hall and knocked at the door of the big bedroom. "Dad?"

"He's downstairs," Rosellen called. "Come in though, Becky, please."

I went in.

Rosellen was sitting on the bed brushing her hair. I asked her, "Where's Hope?"

"She went back to Tacoma. Her father came for her. Her stepmom is out of the hospital and they wanted her there with them."

"How's Nelopie?"

"Doing just fine, gaining weight steadily, they'll be able to bring her home soon."

"That's great."

"Yes, it is."

Then I told Rosellen, "Hope forgot her hat."

"That's okay, she'll be back in August, she can get it then. Becky, you look really sad. What's wrong?"

I couldn't tell her.

Rosellen thought it was just that I didn't have a chance to say good-bye to Hope. She said, "Call her up. She'd like that. I'm sure she's not asleep yet." She gave me the number. "You can use the phone in here. I'll be downstairs."

First I went and got the hat. Then I dialed the number. "Hello, this is Becky Suslow. May I please speak to Hope?"

Hope came on. "Hello, Becky, is it really you?" She sounded surprised that I was calling her up.

"Yes, it's me. You forgot your hat."

"I didn't forget it, I just left it there. It's no good. It doesn't work. I don't believe in it any-more."

"How come?"

"Because you wouldn't make sweet-and-sour Midnight Soup. Because you made me go out of your room."

The way she said it made me feel like a louse. I hated feeling like that. I put the hat on my lap and ran my hand up and down it. Before I knew

it I was saying, "That's funny, because *I* am starting to believe in it."

"You are? How come?"

"Because it's starting to tell me what you
wished." While I said that, my mind did a replay
of Hope giggling when I'd begged her, "Tell me,
tell me, I'll do anything—" And suddenly I knew
exactly what she'd wished when she wore her
witch's costume, the first time she saw me. Of
course, of course, how come I didn't guess sooner?

"You mean the *hat*'s telling you what I wished?"
Hope took a deep breath. "Really, no fooling?"

"Well, I tapped on it three times, and then I
knew, and I didn't know before. And guess what,
your wish came true."

"How do you mean?"

"Come on, you know perfectly well."

She made me say it: "I'll be your friend. That's
what you wished, isn't it?"

I could hear her swallow. Then, in this little
voice, "Yes."

"Well, I want to. D'you believe me?"

"I don't know."

"I'll prove it to you."

"How?"

I was holding the hat. Maybe that's what made

me say, "I got you a present." Because I didn't know ahead of time that that's what I would say.

"You did? What is it?"

"You'll see next time you come."

"No, I can't wait that long, tell me now!"

"Okay. It's a beautiful glass ball. It has a little mountain and a tiny house inside, and snow on the ground. When you shake it, it makes a snow-storm."

"Oh, I love things like that! I can't wait to see it!"

"I'll leave it on your bed. Next to the hat."

"Thanks, thanks, thanks! Wait, Becky, don't hang up yet. Would you do me a favor, even though it sounds dumb?"

"What?"

"Pretend you're first starting to call me up. You say, 'Hello, who's this?' Then I say, 'Hope.' Then you say, 'Hope who?' "

"No. Not another phone trick."

"Come on, please?"

"Okay. Hello, who's this?"

"Hope."

"Hope who?"

"Hope I'll see you real soon! Oh, Becky, I mean it! I really wish it'll happen."

"Yeah. Me, too. Well, so long."

And she said, "Not *too* long. Thanks for calling me. And for the present. I'm really happy now."

Later, when I was in bed, I smelled Dad's oil-paints. I hadn't fallen asleep yet. Too much was happening in my head: Mount Hood, my talk with Hope, and flying home the next morning, seeing Mom, and Michael, and Mrs. Galloway, and my cat Debbie, everybody . . .

When the paint smell got stronger I went down-stairs.

The living room was pretty dark, with only one lamp on, near the easel. Dad stood there and painted. "Well, Boodle, what do you think?"

Most of the canvas was covered with black, dark blue, and dark, dark purple. Up near the top there was a sliver of brightness. It was the moon. And just below it, the white brushstrokes coming to a peak—Mount Hood, with snow, in the night.

"It's getting good," I said, and I watched him paint.

After awhile he asked, "Do you want to put in anything?"

"You mean it?"

"Sure, or I wouldn't have asked. Here's a clean brush you can use."

I looked at the canvas a long time. I started to sense where the lodge would be and where the paths would start. I stuck the brush in the purple paint. "I got too much paint on it."

Dad handed me a rag to take some off. Then I painted some lines leading away from the lodge. They were supposed to be the first path we took. They didn't show up too well, so I added a little bit of white to the purple. Then I put in a dark gray, roundish shape. It wasn't too easy to see.

Dad wrinkled his forehead, looked at it from different angles, and then recognized it. "It's the rock we sat on. Good. It looks right."

In the morning we drove to the airport. Rosellen came along. Both of them hugged me.

Then I got on the plane and flew home.